The WISE WASHERMAN

A Folktale from Burma

Deborah Froese

Illustrated by Wang Kui

Hyperion Books for Children
New York

Printed in Hong Kong.

FIRST EDITION

1 3 5 7 9 10 8 6 4 2

The illustrations are prepared using goauche and watercolor.
This book is set in 16-point Garamond.

Library of Congress Cataloging-in-Publication Data
Froese, Deborah L.
The wise washerman / Deborah L. Froese : illustrated by Wang Kui—1st ed.
p.   cm.
Summary: When the king asks him to wash a gray elephant white, a clever washerman outwits
his jealous neighbor and proves the value of hard work and intelligence.
ISBN 0-7868-0291-X (trade)—ISBN 0-7868-2232-5 (lib. bdg.)
[1. Folklore—Burma.] I. Wang, Kui. ill. II. Title.
PZ8.1.F9235Wi 1996
398.2'0951'02—dc20
[E]   96-33976

ong ago in Burma, Washerman Aung Kyaing (Ahoong Ky-ang) bent over his steaming laundry tub, rubbing and scrubbing the clothes that were brought to him. Everyone believed that he worked magic in his washtub, for he made white clothes gleam like the snowcapped mountains and colorful clothes sparkle like jeweled pagodas. Aung Kyaing was happy to have the admiration of the people but knew that hard work was responsible for his success.

Potter Narathu (Nair-a-thoo), Aung Kyaing's neighbor, watched with a jealous heart. "My neighbor is richer and has a better house," he said. "How is it that he is so much better off than I am? Look how he plays in water and sings happy songs all day. I work just as hard to make my clay pots but no one ever appreciates my efforts." Narathu stared at the lump of clay in front of him but decided that it was too hot to do any work. Instead he stretched out in the shade and began to plot against Aung Kyaing.

Narathu knew that he must be cunning, for he did not wish to anger the king, Pagan Min (Pa-gan Meen), who trusted only Aung Kyaing with the royal laundry. After spending many hours brooding over the situation, Narathu suddenly had an idea that would ruin his neighbor's reputation while making himself appear important in the eyes of the king. The potter dressed carefully in his finest silk *longyi* (long-yee) and wrapped his head in bright strips of silk, hoping to make the best impression. He chose a gift of the most splendid pottery in his shop and set out to request an audience with the king.

After being brought before Pagan Min, Narathu spoke:

"Noble Lord of One Thousand Elephants," he said, "you are a great king and worthy of fine things."

"Ahhh," said the king, who liked a compliment. "I do enjoy fine things. And are they not everywhere around me?" He pointed to his glittering throne, jeweled crown, and golden umbrella.

"Oh yes," Narathu agreed, "almost everywhere."

"Almost!" the king exclaimed, standing up from his throne. "Where is perfection lacking?"

"Well, Exalted One," hesitated Narathu, feigning meekness. "If I might beg your pardon, it's your elephant."

"What's wrong with my elephant?" roared the king.

"It's gray, Your Highness. All the legendary kings in history rode white elephants. Surely you deserve one, too."

Everyone knew that Pagan Min desired a white elephant. Though no one had actually seen one, the creature was a symbol of great importance. Bags of rubies and gold coins were offered to any jungle hunter who could bring such a beast to Pagan Min.

"I know how you can get a white elephant," continued Narathu slyly. "Why not ask Aung Kyaing to wash your gray one? Surely with his magic he can make it white." And when he cannot, he thought, he will be banished from the kingdom forever.

Pagan Min's desire to possess a white elephant overrode his good sense, and he became captivated by Narathu's plan. Immediately he sent a messenger to the washerman to inform him of his command.

Aung Kyaing was dumbfounded. "What shall I do?" he asked. "I cannot make a gray elephant white. But if I refuse to obey the king, he will surely banish me." Hoping to find out more about the situation, he cautiously addressed a few questions to the messenger, who told him all that had happened. The washerman pondered his situation throughout the night. By morning he had come up with a way to try to save himself.

Aung Kyaing put on his best cotton longyi, wrapped his head in strips of cotton, and walked toward the king's palace. When he was presented to Pagan Min, he bowed his head to touch the ground. "O Great King, I am honored by your command, and I will do whatever is within my power to make your gray elephant white. But alas, I cannot succeed at such an important and difficult task unless certain conditions are met."

"What conditions?" the king demanded.

"The Great Wash should take place on the first day of *Thingyan* (Theeng-yan), the Water Festival," Aung Kyaing explained, "the time of washing away the dark deeds of the old year. Everyone in the village brings a water vessel filled with warm soapy water. And of course, Potter Narathu will need to make a clay dish large enough to hold an elephant. The river would be quite unsuitable because the water's flow would carry away my warm soapsuds."

The king, eager to have his white elephant, agreed with everything the washerman requested.

Narathu, when told of the king's command, was unable to refuse. He dug a big hole to make an enormous kiln and collected a pile of clay as high as the roof on his pointed hut. Next he twisted thick coils of clay around and around in the hole to make a huge dish, filled it with straw and palm leaves, and set them on fire in order to bake the clay.

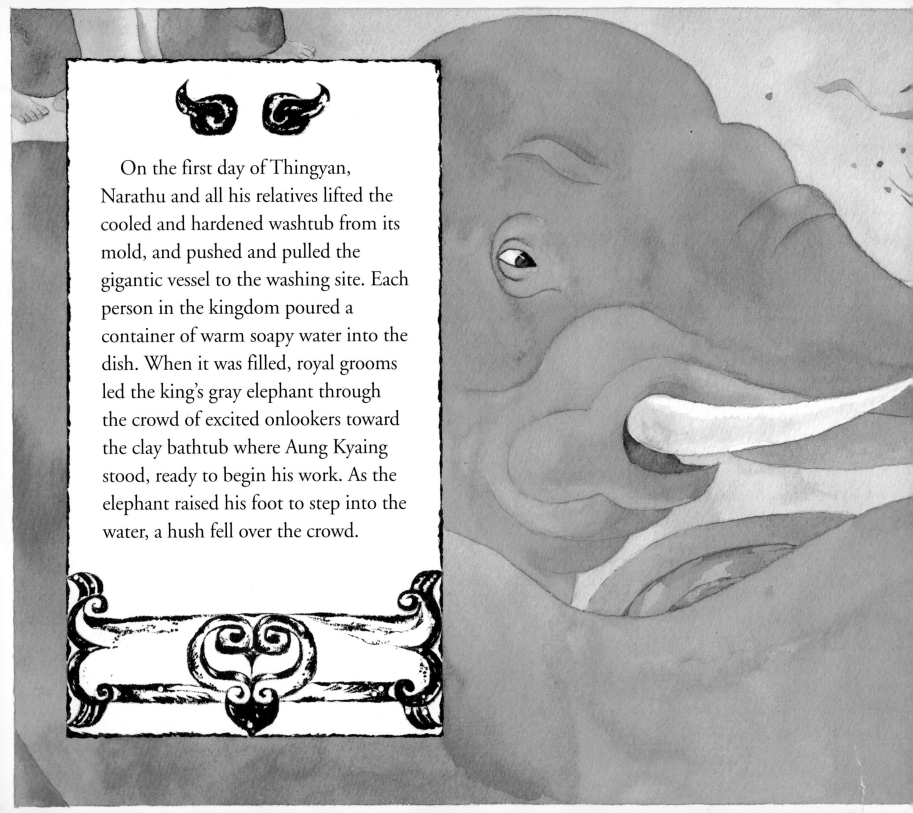

On the first day of Thingyan, Narathu and all his relatives lifted the cooled and hardened washtub from its mold, and pushed and pulled the gigantic vessel to the washing site. Each person in the kingdom poured a container of warm soapy water into the dish. When it was filled, royal grooms led the king's gray elephant through the crowd of excited onlookers toward the clay bathtub where Aung Kyaing stood, ready to begin his work. As the elephant raised his foot to step into the water, a hush fell over the crowd.

But when the creature's heavy foot was lowered into the center of the dish, there was a thunderous crack. The dish shattered, sending a torrent of water over Pagan Min, Aung Kyaing, and everyone nearby.

"You!" Pagan Min roared angrily, pointing at Narathu. "What kind of potter makes an elephant dish that won't hold an elephant? Begone! I send you into the northern hills to live in exile."

Of course, without a dish, Aung Kyaing explained that he couldn't properly perform his task of washing the elephant. So Pagan Min sadly resigned himself to riding his gray elephant in the holiday parade.

After Thingyan, Aung Kyaing resumed his life over his washtubs. He had received so much attention during the Great Wash that many more people brought clothes for him to launder. Yet he couldn't help feeling sorry for Narathu. What would become of him? The man had made good pots but he was never content with his talent.

Knowledge of Burma, legend or otherwise, has been difficult to obtain over the years, for it has remained a relatively closed nation by today's standards. Journalists have been denied access to information or refused entry by government officials. Until recently, visa permits were granted only for visits of seven days' duration.

Burma has more than 120 different ethnic groups spread over an area larger than Alberta, Canada, but smaller than Texas. It is a land of contrasts. There are mountains and river valleys, tropical forests, lush lowland areas, and vast stretches of land prone to drought between rainy seasons. Rural landscapes are often peppered with crumbling, centuries-old pagodas, while urban skylines are capped with gold-leafed, jewel-encrusted temples, evidence of the Buddhist faith that is practiced by the majority of Burmese.

Residents of large urban areas have more modern homes, but the rural population still lives in houses of bamboo walls and thatched roofs. There is no electricity. Each village has a shared central well where people draw their drinking water.

One of the most popular yearly events is Thingyan, the Water Festival, roughly translated to "changeover." It is a three-day event occurring at the height of the hot and dry season in mid-April, when temperatures can soar to over 100°F. This festival celebrates the arrival of the Burmese New Year. Anyone who dares to venture out in the streets during this time is sure to be doused with water—by any means, from water balloon to bucket to fire hose—to wash away the misdeeds of the old year.

Thingyan has become a colorful affair complete with parades and unique forms of theater. Burmese theater, or *pwes* (pways), is a marathon event of drama, singing, dancing, and joke telling. Audiences of all ages gather on mats in front of outdoor stages. Blankets, flasks of tea, and snacks of roasted peanuts or spiced fruit are brought along or purchased from street vendors for much-needed sustenance. Pwes can run all day and night, with those in attendance napping from time to time.

In the midst of the fun, traditional Thingyan rites have not been forgotten. Young people wash the hair of their elders; Buddha images are ceremoniously cleansed; and monks, or *phongyi* (pong-yee), are given special food offerings. These rites are practiced today as they were long ago. And the white elephant is still thought of by many Burmese as something magical, but unfortunately the beast has never been found.